Arthur Starter Book 10

# ARTHUR'S
## Jelly Beans

by Marc Brown

Long tail Books

“Welcome to my Spring Fling party!” Muffy announced. “The first game we’re going to play is—”

“Wait!” said Fern. “Where’s Arthur?”

“There he is,” said the Brain.
Francine sighed. “He’s so slow.”
“Arthur makes turtles look fast,” Buster agreed.
“Hi,” said Arthur. “Am I late?”

Muffy blew her whistle. "Let the games begin!"
First came the Egg Push. Eggs went rolling all over the place.
Binky nudged his into the basket first. Arthur was last.
"With a nose like yours, you should have been first," said Francine.

Next came the Bunny Hop.
"Ouch! My foot!" cried Fern.
Francine hopped across the finish line first.
Arthur was last.

"Is it time for refreshments yet?" Buster asked.

"Almost," said Muffy. "The final game is the Jelly Bean Hunt. Whoever collects the most jelly beans wins the grand prize!"

"What's the grand prize?" asked Binky.

Muffy smiled. “Ta-da! And it’s solid chocolate.”
“Whoa,” whispered the others.

"I want that chocolate egg," Binky said.
"Who says you're going to win?" said the Brain.
"I view my chances as excellent."
"Mine, too," said Arthur.

The other kids looked at each other. Then they burst out laughing.

"What's so funny?" asked Arthur.

Francine said, "It's just that you're so—"

"SLOW!" everyone chimed in.

Muffy passed out paper bags. "You have fifteen minutes to collect the jelly beans. Ready, set, GO!"

"Out of my way!" shouted Buster.

"Winner coming through!" cried Francine.

Everyone raced around the yard. Everyone except Arthur. He hardly moved at all.

"I've already got four!" Fern yelled.
"Try six!" said the Brain.
"One!" said Arthur. "I've got one!"

"My bag is getting full," said Francine.
"I'm going to need a calculator to compute my total," the Brain said.
Muffy checked her stopwatch.
"Six more minutes!" she yelled.

"Can't we just start counting?" asked Buster. "There can't be that many jelly beans left."

"Yeah," said Binky. "I was like a vacuum cleaner. I sucked up all the jelly beans in my path."

"No way!" said Arthur. "I'm still looking."

"Rules are rules," Muffy said. "Five more minutes!"

Buster looked at his bag of jelly beans. *I have so many*, he thought. *It couldn't hurt to eat just one.* Binky saw Buster eating a jelly bean. *If Buster can spare one, so can I*, he figured.

Before long, Fern was dipping into her bag, too.
Then Francine. Then the Brain.

"Are these blue ones cotton candy?" asked Fern.

"I think so, and the brown ones are root beer," said Binky.

"Why aren't there any pink ones?" Francine asked.

Muffy blushed. "I ate all the pink ones before the party."

Then she looked down at her stopwatch.

"Oops! Time's up!" she called.

Everyone lined up and poured out their jelly beans.
Muffy walked down the line counting.
"Fern . . . seven. The Brain . . . six.
Three for you, Binky . . . and nine for Francine."
Then she came to Arthur.

"One, two, three," Muffy began. She kept counting.
"Twelve, thirteen, fourteen. Arthur, you won!"
"I DID?" said Arthur.
"He DID?" said Francine.

Muffy handed Arthur the big chocolate egg.
"I hope you'll all help me eat this," Arthur said.
"Really?" said Buster.
"Of course!" said Arthur.
"I could never finish it. After all . . ."

"You know how slow I am!"